RORY
and his
Shooting Star

THE RORY STORIES ™

D1331175

Author: Andrew Wolffe   Illustrator: Tom Cole

Text and illustrations copyright © Keppel Publishing, 2001
The Rory Stories is a Trademark of Keppel Publishing
First Published 1999.
This edition published 2001.
ISBN: 0 9534949 1 8

A CIP catalogue record for this book is available from the British Library.

Printed in Singapore

KEPPEL
PUBLISHING

Keppel Publishing Ltd.
The Grey House, Kenbridge Road,
New Galloway, DG7 3RP, Scotland.

Includes free RORY STORIES character to cut out and collect.

The sun had long since slipped out of the sky. While he was waiting for his Dad to come and read him a bedtime story, Rory and his little dog, Scruff McDuff, looked out of the window. From his house high above the beach in the village of Sandy Bay, Rory could see for miles around.

Rory could even see all the way down to the beach where he and Scruff McDuff play and have amazing adventures.

Then he looked up to watch the stars sparkling like diamonds overhead and say good night to the man in the moon.

Suddenly, a long streak of silver light flew across the sky with a loud WHOOSH!

"Wow!, what was that?" asked Rory while Scruff McDuff barked and thumped his tail with excitement.

J ust then Rory's Dad came into the bedroom
to read him a story. "Look Dad," said Rory excitedly,
pointing at the strange sight which was lighting up
the sky. "What is it?"

"It's a shooting star," replied Dad. "It's wonderful," gasped Rory, who didn't want to take his eyes off the shooting star in case it vanished into thin air. "Look how fast it's moving. If it doesn't slow down, it's going to run out of sky."

Sure enough, that's exactly what seemed to be happening as the shooting star plummeted closer and closer towards the ground.

"It's heading for the beach," exclaimed Rory. "I wonder where it will land?"

Then the shooting star gave a final burst of dazzling light and seemed to sink behind some rocks which Rory knew like the back of his hand.

The next day Rory and Scruff McDuff ran straight to their favourite rock pool. Rory was sure that was where the shooting star had landed. But when he got there and looked around, all he could see were some shells and a straggly piece of seaweed.

"I wonder what happened to the shooting star, Scruff McDuff?" asked Rory as they climbed over the other side of the rocks. "Maybe," he said sadly, "it broke into a million pieces when it fell out of the sky and now there's nothing left to see."

Just then Rory and Scruff McDuff met a crab scuttling quickly across the sand. "Excuse me," said the crab indignantly, "you're blocking my path."

"Sorry Mr Crab," apologised Rory. "We're looking for a shooting star which fell from the sky last night. Have you seen it?"

"No," replied the crab. "But I did see a bright flash just before I went to bed. It came from over there."

So Rory and Scruff McDuff continued their search. Soon they met a seal relaxing by the side of a rock pool.

"We're in a hurry to find a shooting star which fell from the sky last night," explained Rory. "Have you seen it?"

"Maybe I did, maybe I didn't," replied the seal. "All I know is that a flash of bright light woke me up from a lovely deep sleep."

Next Rory met a seagull standing nearby on top of a post. "I saw the shooting star land right there," said the seagull helpfully. "The bright light it gave off as it fell on to the sand helped me find my new nest."

"I'm sure we're on the right trail," Rory said to Scruff McDuff as they walked towards the spot the seagull had shown them. But still they didn't find the shooting star.

Rory was thinking about what to do next as he walked along the beach. Instead of looking where he was going, Rory was watching the waves wash over the pebbles and listening to the lovely sound they were making.

Even Scruff McDuff was too busy sniffing around to warn Rory about the piece of driftwood that tripped him up.

As Rory lifted his head, he noticed something strange lying right in front of his nose. He sat up quickly and carefully lifted it. The mysterious object was very light and had five fat fingers pointing in all directions. Rory had a good look at it then realised what a wonderful discovery he had made.

"Look what I've found Scruff McDuff," Rory called excitedly.

The little dog trotted over to see what all the fuss was about.

"It's the shooting star that fell from the sky last night," explained Rory.

"I knew we would find it on the beach," Rory said happily. "I'm going to take it home and find a safe place to keep it," he added, gently putting the shooting star into his pocket.

"What treasure have you found on the beach today?" asked Rory's Mum when he and Scruff McDuff arrived back home.

"It's the shooting star that fell from the sky last night," Rory whispered. "It's magical. But we have to hide it or everyone else will want one."

So Mum worked some magic of her own and found the perfect place to keep Rory's shooting star safe.

Now every night, before he closes his eyes and drifts off to sleep, Rory can look up and see his special star, as if it's flying high in the sky and twinkling just for him.

Cut out and keep Rory's special star to add to your collection of characters from THE RORY STORIES.